panda series

**PANDA books are for first readers
beginning to make their own way
through books.**

Granny Makes a Mess!

BRIANÓG BRADY DAWSON

Pictures by Michael Connor

THE O'BRIEN PRESS
DUBLIN

First published 1999 by The O'Brien Press Ltd.,
20 Victoria Road, Dublin 6, Ireland
Tel. +353 1 4923333 Fax. +353 1 4922777
e-mail books@obrien.ie
Web www.obrien.ie
Reprinted 2000

ISBN: 0-86278-612-6

2 3 4 5 6 7 8 9 10
00 01 02 03 04 05 06

British Library Cataloguing-in-publication Data
Dawson, Brianog Brady
Granny makes a mess. - (O'Brien pandas; bk. 13)
1. Children's stories
I. Title
823.9'14 [J]

The O'Brien Press receives
assistance from

The Arts Council
An Chomhairle Ealaíon

Typesetting, layout, editing: The O'Brien Press Ltd.
Cover separations: C & A Print Services Ltd.
Printing: Cox & Wyman, Ltd.

Can YOU spot the panda
hidden in the story?

Danny looked at
his little sister.
Susie was messing
with her dinner.

'Hurry up, Susie,' said Danny.
'Granny is coming to babysit.
I wonder what treats
she'll bring for us!'

When Granny arrived
she gave Danny a
very tight hug.
Then she gave him a
big sloppy kiss.

Yuck! He wiped his face.

Soon Mum and Dad left.
Granny sat down
in the sitting room.

Danny waited for his treat.

He waited and waited.

But Granny said:

'I'm very tired, Danny.

I'm going to rest for a while.

Will you tidy the table?

And keep an eye on Susie.'

Then Granny closed her eyes.

Danny went into the kitchen.
The table was a **mess**!

There were peas
on Susie's chair.
Her soother was
swimming in her cup.
Her bib was covered in goo!
'Susie eats like a pig,'
said Danny crossly.

'Yuck!' he said.
'I'm not cleaning up
this **mess**!
No way!'

Then Danny tripped over
the laundry basket.
The dirty clothes fell out.
'Oh no,' said Danny.
'**More mess**!'

Danny picked up
the laundry basket.
It was empty now.

Then he had a great idea!

He pushed Susie's
sloppy dish
into the middle
of the table.

Then he pushed in
all the dirty plates.

He pushed in
the dirty knives and forks.
He pushed in
the milk jug
and the gravy jug.

Everything was
in the middle of the table.

Then Danny lifted
the corners of the tablecloth.
He made a big bundle.

He dragged the bundle
to the edge of the table.
It was very heavy.
He stuffed the whole lot
into the laundry basket.

Bingo!

The table was clean!

Danny was very pleased.

'Did you see that, Susie?'
he said. 'Amazing!'

But now
the dirty clothes
were all over
the floor.

'I can get rid of
this mess too!'
said Danny.
'Watch this, Susie!'

Danny opened the door
of a cupboard.
It was full of saucepans.
He lifted the lids.
He stuffed dirty clothes
into the saucepans.
He put the lids back on.

'Easy peasy!' said Danny.

But there were more clothes
to get rid of.

Danny picked up

Dad's dirty socks.

He picked up

Susie's messy bibs.

'**Disgusting**!' said Danny.

Susie laughed.

Danny went over
to the bin.
He tossed the dirty clothes in.
'**Gone**!' he said. '**All gone**.'

Next Danny picked up
his dirty football shorts.
He picked up
his dirty pyjamas.
He held his nose.
'**Stinking**!' he said.

Danny looked
around the kitchen.
The bin was full.
The saucepans were full.

'I know,' he laughed.
'**The fridge**!
That will keep them fresh!'

Danny opened the fridge door.
He saw two plastic
vegetable boxes.
Danny opened the
vegetable boxes.

He took out
carrots and cabbage.

He took out
mushrooms and tomatoes.

He took out
broccoli and lettuce.

'We have
too many vegetables
in this house,'
said Danny.
'I hate vegetables!'

Danny stuffed the dirty clothes
into the vegetable boxes.
He put the boxes
back in the fridge.
He closed the fridge door.

No more dirty clothes.

Then Danny picked up
all the vegetables.
'I'll put these where
Mum and Dad
will **never** find them!'
he laughed.
'No more vegetables.
Yippee!'

He went upstairs
to Susie's room.

He put the carrots
in a drawer.

He put the tomatoes
under Susie's cot.

Then he put
the rest of the vegetables
in Susie's wardrobe.

Done! All done!
No more vegetables.
No more dirty clothes.
No more messy table.

Danny smiled
and went downstairs.

Granny was standing
in the kitchen.
She was smiling too.
'I can't believe it!' she said.
'You did a great job, Danny.
Good boy. I'll have
a lovely treat for you
when I've put Susie to bed.'

Susie was very tired.
She began to cry.
'Waaaaaaaah!' she cried.

Granny looked for
Susie's soother.
She couldn't find it anywhere.
'Danny, was Susie's soother
on the table?' she asked.

Oops! thought Danny.

Now, where was that soother?

(In the laundry basket, that's where.)

What will I do? thought Danny.

He said nothing.

Granny searched and searched.

Susie screamed and screamed.

'**Waaaaaaaaaaaaahhhhh**!'

'Granny,' said Danny at last.

'I think it might be in
the laundry basket.'

'Well!' said Granny.

'What a silly place for it.'

Granny turned the laundry
basket on its side.
Out spilled
the dirty
dinner plates.

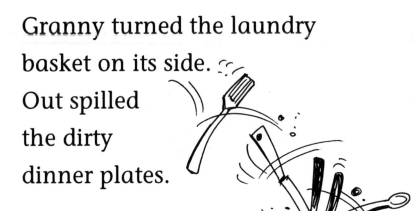

Out spilled
the dirty knives and forks.

Out spilled
the milk jug and
the gravy jug.

Susie was covered
in sloppy dinner.
'**Waaaah**! **Waaaah**!'
she screamed.

'Hush, Susie,' said Granny.
'I'll get some nice warm
milk for you.'
Granny went to
the cupboard.

She took out a saucepan.
She lifted the lid and saw
dirty clothes inside.

Granny opened the fridge door.
She found Danny's
dirty pyjamas in there.
Then she found his
dirty football shorts.

'Disgusting!' said Granny.
She threw the dirty clothes
on the floor.
The kitchen was a mess again!

'This house is a **mess**!'
said Granny.
'And Susie is a **mess**!'
Granny went upstairs
to get clean clothes for Susie.
Danny followed her.

Granny went into
Susie's bedroom.
Danny peeped around
the door.

Granny opened
Susie's wardrobe.

Out fell **cabbage**,
broccoli and **lettuce**.
'Good heavens!' said Granny.
She closed the door quickly.

Then Granny opened a drawer.
'Who put carrots in here?'
she said.

'Oh dear, oh dear,'
said Granny.
'What's going on?'

Then Granny went
over to Susie's cot.
Suddenly she slipped.
She landed on some tomatoes.
She made a big mess
on the floor.
'**Help**!' said Granny.

Danny ran downstairs.
He hid under the table
in the kitchen.

Soon Mum and Dad
came home.
They came into the kitchen.
They saw the **big mess**
everywhere.

'**Danny**!' yelled Mum.

'**Danny**!' yelled Dad.

Danny crept out from
under the table.

'Did you make this mess,
Danny?' said Dad.

'No,' said Danny.
'Granny did it!'

'Granny made a **big mess** in the kitchen.
She made a **big mess** upstairs too.'

Then Granny came
into the kitchen.
'Can I have my treat now,
Granny?' said Danny.

'Treat!' yelled Granny.
'Here's your treat!'
Granny gave Danny
a big cloth.
'You can clean up this mess!'
she yelled. 'Fast!'

Mum and Dad looked cross.
'No treats for you, Danny,'
said Dad, 'for a
whole month!'

'And you'll clean the kitchen
every day,' said Mum, 'for a
whole month!'
'Oh no!' said Danny.

'I'll never do anything
like this again.
Never. Never. Never.'

But I think he will, don't you?
Danny's just that kind of kid.